JAD'S DAD MILO

By John Wilmes

Cover art by Ali Chisatz
Cover format by Nina Azad

Published by Mouse House Books
www.mousehousebooks.com

ISBN 978-1-945327-12-4

The voluptuous, disgusting bass notes of Jad's music fully divided the already barely coexisting halves of the party, "shredding" the floor of the event—as Jad would have it—into two distinct groups.

On one side, Jad's, they were really slapping each other on the back about the music. They jumped about with merciless joy, admiring each other's terrible motions; they would have called their movement dancing, but it definitely wasn't dancing. They grinned and they shouted. "This is fucking dope as shit," one of Jad's friends said, as he high-fived Jad.

The other half of the party, the host's half, was very upset and very quiet. They stewed in their reserved anger, timidly walking toward the stereo every few minutes in the pretense of turning the volume down, but they never made it more than halfway across the room.

One of them, the party's host, Milo, whispered to me about this circumstance, working his way up to a grandstand for all to hear:

"I don't have the words for this situation," he said. "What is that sound effect they're using? Is it *lasers*? I do not find lasers enjoyable, but if Jad and our guests do, I suppose we ought to let them enjoy it. Yes, no, well… *yes*—I would very much like for their enjoyment to be less frightening, to be not so reckless in its hurricane of limbs and epithets and threats, but what do I know about the morality of partying? I've not lost brain cells, willfully, and not with such tremendous exuberance; this destruction of the limited brain—no, I've not done that for years and years. But I used to once, and I can say with certainty that I, too, have disturbed the hosts of my fervor in past days. I used to do a kind of dance. Yes, once, when I was on an acid bender and drunk as all shit, I crawled in front of dozens of people to scream hyperboles about capitalism, about 'the knives of the dollar sign killing all the misfits,' so I do know I've been a nuisance to well-intentioned company before. But it's been a while since I felt enough pain to rage like that. I only want to be reasonable, now. I turned thirty years old, and for years and years after I have only wanted to be reasonable. That's where I find God: in my reasons. They find theirs in their partying, I find mine in my reasons. Every concept I can use to effectively validate my actions, consider that a 'beer downed.' In fact, I even sometimes say 'beer me' when I realize my behavior aspires toward larger, benevolent theories of living. That's how I get 'juiced,' these days; on self-congratulation, in the name of my bastard religion, composed of disparate ideas that tickle me so. 'I've got the power of karma on my back, boosting me through,' I'll say, taking stock of the healthy forty percent I always tip my delivery drivers, my taxi cabs, my waiters and my waitresses. I'm paying a cosmic tax, I'm buying my security, I believe, and how is that not as sinful as what these young boys are doing here? At least their bit is entertaining—mine is just a spit at my discomfort with the class system. But of course, yes, of course, to me in my happy moments, my increasingly frequent happy moments, this relatively small expenditure is in fact no spitting, it is no malicious gesture at my unease with the burning, unfair world, no, it is a spiritual embrace of other folks. It is a holy good, this tipping policy, so consider me beered, consider me drunk on the optimism of my actions. It is only in my present state, with this *laser music* playing at such volume, with its bass lines so seductively assaulting my senses and rocking me, it is only now that I'm upset enough to take issue with my healthy forty-percent tipping policy. Which, of course, I should be commended for," Milo said, turning a bit red.

Milo then approached Jad, his son, and Jad's friends. He shouted "forty percent" at them. "Forty percent!" he screamed over the laser music, and he grabbed a vase off his kitchen table and aggressively stepped toward the volume knob, making many motions as if to hurl the vase while walking—but he never, in fact, let go of the vase as he swung it. He turned the volume of the laser music down and spun around, pointing at Jad and his friends with the vase like it was a lecture stick, leaning toward them. "Forty percent!" he said. "That's what I tip my service people! I say hello to strangers, even if I don't know them. Citizenship!" he screamed, shaking the vase at them. He stroked the vase downward into the air repeatedly, as if he were a judge, banging a gavel. He shouted "citizenship," again and again. "This is not citizenship, what you are doing. It's war! And I do not appreciate you staking a flag of opposition in my own home, and it's high time I did something about it!"

Milo smashed the vase over his countertop and ran at Jad with a jagged fragment of it, and Jad kept saying "bro, please, chill out," but Jad's father Milo swiped at his son's abdomen with the vase fragment anyway. Jad, however, was much larger, and he caught his father's forearm and squeezed it. "Bro," he said, "you gotta chill out. We got plenty of drugs here for everyone. Don't worry, man."

Milo, nearly crying amid the pain his son was applying to his forearm, reluctantly rested the jagged vase fragment onto the table beside him. Jad and his friends put on new music, far more mellow fare with a harmonica and standing bass, and they swept up the mess of vase, diligently putting it into the trash and clearing the coffee table for at least a dozen lines of cocaine.

Jad sniffed up some of the cocaine, Milo sniffed some, I sniffed some, everybody sniffed some and then we were all arguing about sports, gesturing wildly as our body heat rose and we splashed spittle on each other and laughed more than is said to be alright by doctors. "We're totally crushing it now," Jad kept saying, and he gave me a high-five that I felt for days.

Jad eventually felt chummy enough toward me to explain how his father Milo, my employer, could be this way sometimes. He said it all had to do with *his* father, Jad's grandfather, and the way he was always saying everything was a lesson, even the worst events in life, the ones that were in fact pure tragedy, moments absent of God and love and meaning, like when a stranger broke into the host's house, Jad's father Milo's house, once, when Milo was thirteen years old. The stranger, Jad said, shot Milo's dog Frankie to death and left without touching another thing, without stealing anything.

"See," Milo's father then told him, after the shooting. "This is all a lesson. Frankie wouldn't have met such a fate if he had been more smartly protected. Frankie doesn't like these loose locks, these loose locks you leave after you play in the yard with him so close to the nighttime, Frankie gets hurt and dies when you leave such big openings into the house, and so could your father, too. I might die and so might you soon, too, if you keep leaving these loose locks around here."

Milo's father, Jad told me, was a broad and towering man who moved gently, always gently, but only because he never needed to move forcefully because beyond being physically terrifying, he was mentally terrifying. When you played chess with him, he'd always tell you he was at least fourteen moves ahead of you, the way Jad told it, and it was hard not to believe his calculation with the way that he always won. "Still fourteen moves ahead," he'd say, with extreme calm, according to Jad, and then he'd kill everything with his bishop and drink his spiked milk. He'd tap you on your shoulder, when he was done, with the heft of a pillow. "Try to get it under fourteen," he'd say, emoting nothing.

Once, Jad told me, Milo's father had a tap-dance performance and Milo and all of his family were forced to go to it—Jad was always calling his father "Milo" in these stories, never "my father," or "my dad," and Milo's father was usually curiously referred to as "pap," a disgustingly sentimental noun. Milo's father, the enormous pap, moved like a cloud at the tap-dance performance, like an oversized cloud made of rocks and titanium that defied physics by doing these dances, by affecting the ground beneath him so little, he wouldn't even leave a dustprint with the way that he moved. Milo's father's smile, Jad said, was almost entirely imperceptible—"I could figure out when that bro was happy only by the time I turned eighteen. And when I looked back on shit from all my life, I figured out Milo's pap was real happy, happier than ever, when he did that dance and the dance made him look real tiny and agile for a minute, like a special weightless critter."

After the dance, Jad said, he saw Milo's father walking comfortably out of the building, a school, entirely satisfied in appearance. He said Milo trailed a minute later holding his heart, trembling and nearing a breakdown.

Jad and I did more cocaine and sat on a couch across the room from everyone, observing his father, Milo. "His pap was real messed up but so is he, too," Jad said. He said the vase incident of tonight was a story that probably wouldn't even last two weeks between him and his friends, it simply wasn't remarkable enough. Much more momentous things had happened between the two of them. As Jad did this, as he speculated about the endurance of the evening's mythos, I watched Milo, my employer, whacking his palms to the kitchen countertop with unbridled delight, screaming the name of a basketball player. "Nikola Mirotic!" he said, over and over. "Nikola Mirotic!"

Jad told me that his father, when Jad observed him while home for the holidays, would coop up in a personal room, well away from Jad and away from Jad's mother, where he had a large television screen and a very expensive miniature basketball hoop on the wall. As the Chicago Bulls played, Milo would run relentlessly about the little room as if it were, itself, the pasture of a professional basketball court. He would imitate the players on his hoop as he watched them, dunking and shooting and rebounding. He'd occasionally leave the room to go to the bathroom and pour himself a very tall, very cold glass of water while sweating profusely and smiling uncontrollably. He'd shout "beer me" as he poured himself the glass of water.

Jad said this party we were at was "one of the tamer January throwdowns" they'd had in ages. At the last one, he said that he, Jad himself, had been going through an awful breakup and Milo wanted too badly to console him through it. "It was pretty chill of Milo to do that," Jad said, "but man, he took it too far. He like, started asking if it was okay if he could hold me. Like, in front of all my dudes. He said his own pap never touched him more than on the shoulder, so soft it almost wasn't a touch, and that his pap could only talk to him through metaphors. If he ever wanted to say 'dude, I love you,' or anything like that, he could only do it through space heaters and vitamins, and he usually wasn't even saying 'dude, I love you,' or anything like that, through space heaters and vitamins. Milo thought he was saying stuff more like 'stop being so unterrifying under the light of the Lord, stop needing these things like my suckling little lamb; learn power'; that's the kind of thing Milo thought his pap was saying to him with that shit. Then he was, you know, Milo was saying in front of all my friends how much he loved me and how much of a 'horrible oil-drinking bitch' my girlfriend, my *ex*-girlfriend was. Milo said she had 'assholes in her eyes and isn't long for the generous half of the world.' Then he just said 'dude, I love you' over and over and in a way that hurt me for a while. He said that 'when the reckoning comes' I could 'live in the warmth of his wings' because he was a father, a real father unlike his, and he said 'dude, I love you' *so* many times and he was crying. That was last January," Jad told me.

As Jad told me this story, the once hilariously crying Milo was in the kitchen pretending to play Russian roulette with Jad's friends, using a small water gun and making theatrical death gestures as they dribbled water onto their temples.

Jad asked me what kind of a boss Milo is, and I told him Milo is a much different boss than he is a father. I told him of how Milo would bring dozens of donuts to the office biweekly, but he'd place them on an empty desk just outside his office, and would watch the surface all day to see who took the donuts. "When he saw you take one, he would resolutely make some kind of mark in a notebook —this became unmistakable after months of it, I doubted my suspicions of this strange system at first but there was no two ways about it, over time it became clear he was keeping a donut consumption inventory. I kept my own inventory once, you see—I opted to work, for one fateful donut day, at an unoccupied desk adjacent to the donut table, which was not normally visible from my office. In my own personal notebook I tallied who took how many donuts, which kinds they took, and when. And I observed in the following week what the consequences were, of Milo's donut consumption inventory. Those who took more donuts were, in fact, rewarded in small ways. For those who took the most donuts, he would very pointedly visit their desks during the following week and tell them how wonderful of a job they'd been doing. He started with the same words every time. 'I can't believe how lucky we are to have you,' he'd always say. He'd then hand them a gift card to an electronics store, a bulk of which was given to him by *his* bosses, to do with what he pleased, and what he was pleased to do with them was distribute them based on donut consumption. I asked him about this once, your father. We were drunk as all shit one day after work, I'd gotten him to that state by capitalizing on an especially heated bout of his ping pong love. I'll get to that in a bit. Drunk as a fucking fool, post-ping-pong-love, though, that's when I confronted him about his donut inventory. I was a bit mad, you see, as I wanted a gift card to the electronic store for a new video camera I'd been eyeing, but he didn't give me a gift card. I refuse to eat donuts, ever, for reasons concerning the body, so it was more than bothersome to me to discover he was managing a department in which donut consumption was secretly rewarded. Anyway, when I brought your father's attention to the issue of his donut inventory and its related reward system, asking many questions about his management ethics, he hedged me and he hedged me, never quite explaining himself, and it then seemed clear to me that Milo operates our department almost entirely based on obscure whims, ones I still can't define—I don't believe this now, for the record. There is something more than whims to his ways; there is a singular, slippery and insane logic that your father uses to run the department, one that involves whims and frivolous tricks but that is also, ultimately, very complicated and difficult to trace in its full-ness.

"'They love the numbers!' your father eventually came to repeat ad infinitum as I pried into his tricks. He said this in reference to his bosses and how he appeased them, despite his bizarre tactics, typified by this donut inventory. He said 'they love the numbers' as if it were the shield to a secret formula, and he loved that shield, he even loudly sang his 'they love the numbers' phrase at one point as he was drunk, to the tune of a song I happened to make love to once, recently, in a loaded way. I'll get to that in a bit, though, because I've still not shed light on this ping pong love I speak of.

"Your father Milo *loves* to play ping pong at the workplace. The curious thing is that he isn't any good at it, you see. I don't think I've ever seen him win a game. But he'll still saunter over to that community table, every two hours, to make sure he gets in some action. He'll giggle as he plays, faltering mightily each and every time. It's rare that he loses by any less than twelve points, usually it's much more. 'Only lost by eighteen this time!' he'll sometimes say with glee. He'll play in a prancing way, comparing himself to Chicago Bulls players as he does so. 'I'm Joakim Noah!' he'll say, moving in more of a dancy fashion than in any way that could be considered competitive, or strategic. He'll pretend to comb the flowing hair he doesn't have when he says he's Joakim Noah. As you know, your father's hair is actually quite short. The ball will jet by him repeatedly as he gallops, signifying more losing. Everyone will crush your father in ping pong, and he couldn't be any happier about it. I envy his way of perceiving something that for me can only cause anger, or can only cause a combative form of joy, at best. Competition, of the socially-accepted kind—to me, this is a matrix of only violent emotions, but for your father this is a place where what I can only call 'play' takes place, and I envy him greatly for his sense of play. Everyone stomps his ass in ping pong repeatedly, and he absolutely adores the experience.

"Everyone, of course, except for Joe. Joe wouldn't be beaten by your father in ping pong, no, those two wouldn't even play. In fact, Joe would win, always, regardless of who was playing. Joe is a superb, arguably unstoppable ping pong craftsman. But your father would always beat him, somehow, in a more important way; he'd smash Joe in the ether where consequences more soulful than ping pong scores occur. Every time Joe actually went to the community table, you see, he won but he only left with pain, and it was always pain caused by your father. For reasons that I can't fully understand, because Joe's been with the department far longer than I have, your father completely despises Joe. When Joe plays ping pong, your father will sit on the recliner near the table and, with great pleasure, he'll distract Joe's opponent with the most lively conversation imaginable. Your father Milo has this wonderful way of completely focusing into whatever's at the forefront of his employees' minds. It is, almost never, work-related—no, not the topic your father uses to distract Joe's ping pong opponents with, it's basically never work-related. Instead he'll bring up the employees' children, their pets, whatever it is they're most eager to talk about—a dating situation, for the single ones. 'How's the sex?' I once heard him ask, he'll stoop even to this level to poke holes into Joe. For the duller, lonelier sorts, it's a hobby like 'wind weaving,' or whatever the *fuck* it is that people do with their time. Your father never asks questions about this shit otherwise. He saves this brand of boss appeal exclusively for when his employees are facing Joe in a round of ping pong. Your father's compartmentalizing this form of appeal—which, to be sure, is completely intoxicating; your father is brilliant at cutting close to the id of his employees—his compartmentalization of this appeal is so extreme that the whole department understands, at least on a subconscious level, that this is how they can talk to their boss about what they most care about: by playing Joe in ping pong. The thing about it is, this sort of distraction actually makes Joe's ping pong games quite easy for him to win. No one plays against Joe in ping pong with any real level of attention, not with the way your father talks to his opponents. And Joe has come to understand your father's sub-surface tactics, I believe, and is thus profoundly dissatisfied by his inability to actually beat, to actually roundly defeat anyone in a round of ping pong. Joe, like me, I believe, perceives and experiences these socially accepted forms of competition as only the host of very violent emotions, rarely any positive ones, and your father's causing of Joe's dissatisfaction by preventing him from any actual competition, this is a great blow delivered by your father. He still manages to keep Joe on enough of a string to have him continually play the game, though—Joe keeps coming back for more torture.

"Your father, in no uncertain terms, *owns* Joe. A former co-worker, Philly, has told me all about their history. Actually, Philly's version of things seems spotty at best, but what I've gleaned from his sloppy tellings, at the very least, is this: your father once eviscerated Joe's very essence with what Philly called 'a vastly destructive dish document.' There's a kitchen at our office, you see, and your father was at one point incredibly unhappy with the state of the kitchen. He would pound his fists against the walls of the kitchen when no one was in it and scream things about the state of the kitchen. 'This is not how you tend to a place where people eat!' he'd scream. 'These dishes are in a way that only a monogoloid would accept! This is a place where taste goes to die! I wouldn't even *hang myself* in a place like this!' The yelling about the state of the kitchen was so disturbing, Jad, that his employees were said to be in denial of it. They all completely ignored it. Your father can be completely, so intolerably kind and composed as our boss, so shining, you see, that the margins in which he totally loses his cool and throws shit at the veritable walls are simply ignored by myself and the rest of us. We'd rather not deal with that rather minuscule part of your father. The rest of him is simply so good. This bottling up of your father's dissonant state, regarding the cleanliness of the office's kitchen, however, eventually led to the destructive document Philly told me about. Your father Milo composed and disseminated this document on the department network. Everyone could see it, as there was a clear link to it on the front page of the department network, which each employee was required to log into at the beginning of every work day. The document was entitled 'Look at what Joe did; from your boss, Milo' and anyone who didn't click on it and also read all of it, the very day it was posted, well, they surely did so by the next day. I actually have the document, right here, it's on my phone."

I took my phone out of my pocket and I opened the document, I showed it to Jad. It looked like this:

[photo of a plate on the kitchen table, covered in hardened barbecue sauce]

Joe not only eats like a nine-year-old, he also keeps after himself like one, as you can see here. Where's mother? Where's mother? She isn't coming, Joe. This is adult life. Wolf down some actual nutrients instead of your disgusting chicken fingers, that unacceptably large, frozen bag of which you keep in the freezer. Some of us may be desiring that space in the freezer for something that isn't merely fuel for a quick decay.

[a photo of the same plate, but in the sink now, with some water over it]

Ah, there it is. There you go, Joe. Water. Ever heard of water? It's a compound element, which means that it's formed from two other elements: two parts hydrogen, one part oxygen. H-Two-Oh. That's what they call it, colloquially, sometimes, but truly most just call it water. Perhaps it comes out of your shower head, but I doubt very much that you know that, based on what we've seen and smelled from you here in this office. Anyway, this miracle compound element serves many, many functions, one of which is that it erodes most edible substances off of glass kitchenware over time—this grotesque non-food sauce of yours included. Wetting your used plate requires a full nine-second exertion, I know, moving the plate to the sink and getting this water substance on it (and no mothers around to help you with the process), but I'm positive that you can do it. Actually, I'm not positive you can accomplish anything at all, but someone hired you for my department, so I'm asking that you move immediately out of your infantile comfort zone, into the sane, big-kid world, and perform this chore for me regularly.

[a photo of an elaborate arrangement of dishes in the sink, with water running slowly over and through them, the dishes together making a complex, winding levee]

See, look. If you use water, you can even have fun with the dishes. This work of mine, this wonderful and temporary structure of dishes—it's structurally sound, pleasing to look at, and effective at keeping our office's dishes cleaned. You can even run the sink at a low, warm rate for minutes on end when you make brooks like these—the water can run through it, streaming as nature intended for water to stream, and so through this dish-cleaning process we can let our ungodly skyscrapers contain this extra semblance of the natural while we live too much in them. This, though, Joe, this handiwork of yours, this is modernity gone terribly wrong:

[a photo of a countertop covered in crumbs and sticky substances, and unwashed dishes]

Here's where you reveal that your understanding of modernity is that it only me-

ans you need not do any work, because your God is simply whatever reason you can muster to justify a lack of personal growth. Scraps everywhere, garbage on the counters: with your mess you're telling me everything I need to know about how you view the world. You think it's a game, not a thing to be maintained with grace, and you think that your mother is around the corner, eager to pick things up. There are no mothers, not one, in this office, Joe. The women who work here and have children, they are not mothers while they are here, they are citizens of this space, and they pick up after themselves only, as should you. I have been your mother, I have cleaned up after you, but I refuse to do it any longer. You misunderstand my role: I am not a mother, I am a government, and now I unleash my police on you in the form of this document. It's time for a tutorial, Joe, because you need to be edified about acceptable cohabiting behavior. So watch this:

[a video is here embedded, in which Milo whistles doo-wop songs to himself and artfully cleans a filthy kitchen, performing the clean as if it were an athletic feat. He clearly takes a measured, scientific approach to his body movement, occasionally muttering clichéd phrases about basketball—"he shoots, he scores"; "Kobe"; "a defiant rejection of Joe's dirty bullshit"; "The defense is suffocating this mess"—and pumping his fist throughout. There is a rhythm to his self-loving method, there is an arrogance to it, there is hate and love in it, but there is also efficiency and craft in it. He knows just what he's doing, even resolving all the hanging notes of his doo-wop melodies as he finishes the whole deed with a flourishing wipedown of the last messy surface. Then he

looks directly into the camera and says "welcome to the delight of adulthood, Joe. I hope you'll join me."]

"Buzz about this dish document grew quickly around the office. Joe's embarrassment, his shame, then became clear once he took a week off from work and ignored all text messages sent to him by co-workers. Many began to question Milo's status as boss, for creating such a flagellating, such an abusive document. *His* bosses, surely, couldn't allow such a thing. But our queries about this, to anyone we asked about it outside of our department, were always met by the confident assurance that the big bosses 'love the numbers' and in time it was clear that there was nothing anyone in the department could do about it, not within the confines of this company. Your father's status as department boss, and his power to do what he did to Joe—we became aware that this was entirely alright with the company, which loved the numbers, and after a week or two, Joe returned and he was visibly uncomfortable for some time, before his rivalry with your father subsided to a level, this ping pong level, which I believe most people in the department forgot about, but which I see so very clearly.

"I was not yet with the company when Joe was obliterated by the dish document, but I knew fully when I saw your father deprive Joe of one of the few satisfactions he could comprehend—one of the rare forms of pleasure Joe could understand, the ping pong form—I knew watching your father do this to Joe that it was an extension of the fury in that largely forgotten document, and I knew also, in seeing this, not to cross your father without great strategy, without great intelligence and mystery.

Your father Milo is a cunning man, he certainly can be despite the front of his agreeability, he is cunning enough to warrant my fear and caution if I were ever to cross him, if I were ever to pursue a desire that conflicted with one of his.

"He would even deny Joe surrogate forms of ping pong achievement, you see, when Joe tried to create them. At one point, Joe began cheering himself up by announcing just how dominant his victories had become, regardless of the fact that your father was controlling his very situation and synthesizing Joe's victory, giving it to him. Joe would say 'twenty-point victory, this time,' with a knowing grin. 'I absolutely *slammed* the ball on at least thirteen of those points,' he'd say. Your father was bothered by that form of scorekeeping for a week or so, I could read it on his face. Milo began to stumble a bit as he asked

Joe's opponents what they cared about. He'd lost his path to the id, he looked eminently frustrated as he searched for the next question, querying Joe's opponents about things as banal as *soda* instead of their domestic lives and their dreams. He was losing his grip on Joe's heart—for a week he could no longer choke Joe's guts into submission.

"But then, on a Monday, your father came in with an emotional hammer. When Joe announced that he was up nineteen-to-zero in a game, on seventeen expedient slams and two trick shots, your father looked at him with the most devious smile I've ever seen in any office. 'Stop quantifying these things,' he said, with a calm and unimpeachable thrust. 'You're quantifying all of the wrong things.' When Joe told him that he was 'only quantifying dominance,' your father laughed at him, and said 'listen, I'm the boss because they love the numbers,' and your father didn't move a muscle. Joe didn't either, and he proceeded to crush his opponents in ping pong. But his ability to find joy in his victories quickly waned. He began telling everyone that he was 'the best' at inappropriate volumes, his words rising to the point that the boss of the department upstairs came down and gave Joe a scolding, a totally humiliating screed that included the words 'lousy loser losing everything, likely to die in a ditch next to nobody dogs and crying like pizza crust,' and Joe slammed the ping pong ball as hard as he could against the wall. He ran out of the room, resembling an incredibly agitated teenager who'd just been told he can't go to a rager, a rager like this one—I'd hate to have you think I'm not enjoying myself, Jad, as I tell you all these stories about your father. And I quite like Milo, too—I'm just saying I wouldn't want to mess with him, is all, and that's an admirable quality of his, especially considering that he is my boss. And I'm surprised, very much, by this side of him you tell me of, by all these dimensions of his identity at home, which are not at all clear at the work place. That's all, Jad," I said. "I'm loving this rager; it's all love," I said, because I believed Jad would like that sort of phrase.

That's when Jad patted me on my back many times, telling me it was "of course all love." He stood from his seat next to mine and put his hand out and I grabbed his hand, and he pulled me up from my seat. We then walked over to the water-pistol Russian roulette game, in the kitchen. Milo handed me the water pistol. I took it from him and envisioned my fake death performance, knowing that Milo would love it wholly.

I'd learned to manipulate Milo almost wholly; I knew just what it was that he liked, even if I often couldn't understand the code by which he ran our department successfully, which I determined he was consciously hiding from me each time I tried to siphon it out of him. He could hide his jigsaw rules of departmental magic from me, and wield his line about "numbers," cruelly, when I tried getting beneath his armor about the department's maintenance—yes, he could. But he could not avoid my charm, my way of pleasing him, and this was what mattered most.

With my charm, I could gradually chip away at whatever it was that was keeping me from the treasures I knew Milo hid in his mind, his secret words and moves that I had to have. So I held the toy pistol and I performed my fake death under the weight of its piddling water, just the way Milo wanted to see it, I knew his wants so well already. Milo was not punchless, to be sure, it had taken me some time to peer into him like I had, but in my charm I'd found the perfectly immobilizing tactic to use against him. I'd had to use much less on men to get my way with them in the past, to be sure, but I'd also had to use much more to disarm a manager before.

I shot the pistol's little stream onto my temple but then also just under my eyes, falling to my knees as I wailed and pretended the water was gross little tears, and I dropped the pistol with great timing. It was all a finely tuned mockery of the dramatic arts, which I knew that Milo didn't respect. I knew that Milo did not respect art, that he only respected sport. I said something about "the death knell of a work promotion"—I'd recently been promoted by Milo, which I loved, but it wasn't enough—and I hit my head gently against the edge of his kitchen's countertop.

Milo cherished my act, he absolutely loved it, and then his wife finally spoke after being subdued all night—the raging had clearly not been to her liking, but very instantaneously it seemed that the partying pleased her as I did my thing. "Wow," she said, laughing a lot, sounding like a perfect idiot, this delicious woman Larissa—I'd only just noticed her. "I've seen Milo do *that* just about a billion times."

Then Larissa left the room. Just as she made herself visible to me for the first time, right as she appeared present, like a bright torch cutting you with feeling in the blackness of the unforgiving abyss of the night, she went away. The light of her went suddenly on, then off, and I was alone again. Larissa didn't return to the room; for months after I didn't hear her amazing and graceless language, her blabbering nonsense that functioned on a level I'd have to describe as "holy," this yammering.

In that very moment, Milo's wife Larissa, Jad's mother, demonstrated such an immaculate embodiment of what I wanted behavior to be that I didn't stop thinking about it, not once, for a six-month period. I did everything I could, without revealing the nervous state Larissa had put me in, to get close to her again.

At first this effort involved, more than anything, befriending Jad. When I left the party that night, doing one final line of cocaine with Jad and Milo before I went down to my taxi, I got Jad's phone number from him and the next day I laid out my plan. My plan involved gaining Jad's affections to a huge degree, making Milo feel as though I was so close with his son that the only way he could be as close to his son as I was would be through a sort of three-way friendship between myself, Jad, and Milo. I would then, somehow, leverage this tension—

the tension of Milo not yet becoming part of this trio, this triumvirate friendship I would trick him into aspiring toward—I could tilt this tension in a way that got Milo on my page in a very petty work grudge. I would somehow use his insecurity over mine and Jad's friendship to nudge him into forming a "sub-kitchen," a specially designed, privileged food area, with boutique grills and dishes that Milo would buy with inappropriate amounts of company money.

I could awaken both an unease in Milo about my relationship with his son Jad, and a version of his old anger about the kitchen situation. The kitchen situation, which led to the destruction of Joe, was the only obvious hole in Milo's office armor, the only one I could see in all my looking. And now that he'd let me into his home, now that he'd made the mistake of welcoming me into "the warmth of his wings," I could stab him just where I wanted to, in that spot he thought no one could see, right in that wound he thought none of his employees would have the guile to poke.

He was wrong, of course. I'd been tempted to stab him right there for a while, but my ceaseless enchantment with his wife Larissa, in her one crazily perfect moment at one party, tipped me over into the deed. I was now holding the veritable needle, just inches from his opened wound, and I would take the time to show him that the needle was there and that there was nothing he could do to make me move it, and that I could push the needle in whenever I decided it was aimed rightly enough.

I'm a patient man, though. Larissa's vagina could never wait half the time for me to penetrate it as I could wait to penetrate; no vagina with my patience exists, and none ever will. I am Bert Britwell, I do everything with design, I don't care about the moments that stack up into bigger moments, not the way that other people do, I see only the grand collection of them. Milo thought he had the strings, he thought he could pull us all in the department, make us do whatever he wanted. But that was before my plan started taking hold of him and his life. I laughed to myself as I left the rager, planning my friendship with Jad. It started with the friendship with Jad—the "sub-kitchen" plan would have to wait until later.

I sent Jad a text message two weeks after the "January throwdown." I asked if he was going to see the band he played for us as we did cocaine at the throwdown—they were playing at the Empty Bottle that night. Jad was all too predictable: he wasn't the type to keep tabs on such calendar items, but he was unquestionably the type to flip his wig about it when it popped up and surprised him. He text messaged me back with many exclamation points, and said he was clearing his schedule and inviting all his friends to see the cocaine band, the one with harmonica and a standing bass, at the Empty Bottle that night. He said he hoped to see me there, and I pumped my fist with malice in my office, the one right next to his father Milo's.

As I expected, that night, Jad gave away information about Milo without my even asking for it. Jad, a poor protector of his father, handed me goodies, insights I could use to climb into his mother's vagina, of which he was also a poor protector. "Milo's the shit," Jad said to me at the show, in a drunken emotional oblivion. "I think, and this is mostly because he's my bro, but I think Milo is probably the best boss you're ever gonna have. You've probably never had a better boss, man. Listen, at

Milo's pap's funeral, you should've *seen* the way that he bossed that shit. I was sad as all hell, dude, and usually Milo's the one to be crying and shit, not me, but he didn't cry, man, just me and my mom, and everyone else cried too, but not Milo. At that funeral, man, he just straight up told this awesome story, during the ceremony, about his pap. He said that he didn't understand objects, not really, without his pap. He couldn't even, like, move around rooms, he said. He'd basically be a blind guy who couldn't even make sense of stuff like furniture and roads, without his pap. His pap, Milo said, was all about 'the moment directly beyond the present, where you get hit.' He said his pap said you could take yourself off of the world if you could notice it rotating beneath you, you could just hum along its surface like a fart of God's, if you wanted to, when you saw things the right way. Man, it was so tight. Milo said he never did see it just that way, he never could quite understand what his giant pap meant with all that, but he said that he only moved in relation to those words. He said he couldn't think about stepping or skipping one inch without feeling the pull of what his pap was teaching him, without feeling that place he tried directing him to."

I hated the story, but I leaned into it nonetheless, of course, while the band played their best song—the one I had once made love to, in a loaded way, but it's still not the time for that tale. I gave Jad my hand, I put it on his shoulder and said how lucky I was to have Milo as a boss. Jad was crying but he was also pumping his fist triumphantly. He turned his attention to chorus of the band's best song, the chorus in which their harmonica was unstoppable.

I took off early that night, I refused Jad's invitation to further drinking at more bars, because I knew not to be hasty in what I was planning, and that I should feel accomplished with this seed I'd so pointedly sown.

The following week, I bought tickets to an especially important Chicago Bulls game, and invited Milo to come with me. He said yes, hugging me like I'd pieced his scattered heart back together when I told him outside of my office. And at the game, he was even more enthusiastic and open. He told me sordid things about him and Larissa, details that made me sweat and wonder what I was in for, but in a positive way—in a way that had me seeing myself like a floating explorer, who realized the mass he was shining his light on in the dark was so much bigger, so much grander and more complex, so much more teeming with unique lifeforms than it previously seemed to be. Milo told me that he and Larissa had come to experiment sexually, as a result of her "goofy tendencies." He said she had grown to enjoy intercourse only if there was "an awfulness to it." I felt myself nearly explode. He didn't go on, though, not right away, because those Bulls started captivating him. "Yes!" he kept saying, watching them make mutton of the other team. "Rose blooms, gold looms! I'm going to marry each and every one of these basketball players, I'm going to take them with me to thc prom and the picnic, I can't stand how much I love this team! These Bulls! These terribly exciting Bulls!" he yelled, patting my shoulders through it all and drinking his bottles of water, saying "beer me" every time the Bulls scored.

It was only after the game, when I managed to get him drunk and dumb, capitalizing this time on his love for the Bulls, that he elaborated on the "awfulness" that Larissa so loved. He said she spit in his mouth a lot during sex, from a distance, and that she expected him to do the same or else she'd start biting him, with a fierceness that went beyond what most would consider sensual. He said she would announce his sexual moves before he made them and she was thrilled when she was right, and that she would orgasm only if her predictions came correct. I had a hard time containing myself: I'd never heard of anything so lovely, so unbelievably enticing. But I held myself in, I proceeded to keep getting drunk as shit with Milo and I kept hearing him out about whatever was on his mind. It was as if he were facing Joe in ping pong, and I were him, cutting right into his id from the recliner on the side of table as Joe achieved his pointless points.

Mostly, however, Milo was interested in talking about the Bulls, announcing to a bar near their stadium, where we were drunk as shit after the game, that "Jimmy Butler is running the fast break on my ass break, he's invading my orifices with this forceful play, I can't believe how much he stampedes! I concede my limbs to him, to Jimmy Buckets, I do!"

I did nothing with my plans for another month. I knew I only needed to let my investments in my design appreciate, to let the seeds I'd planted grow into sticks and little spectacles. Milo's affection for me at the office hit unwieldy heights during that month, as he began giving me more than my fair share of the electronics store gift cards, almost daily. His supply of them was almost infinite, it turned out, and he winked at me as he gave them over and said "Go Bulls" every time. I bought my video camera, the one of my wishes, during that month, and also received a number of text message invitations from Milo's son Jad, who was quite taken with me, because—I deduced —of how I enabled him to talk about his father. I rebuffed those advances from Jad, though, knowing that I could bring him and his father together at my apartment, later, at my annual Saint Patrick's Day bash. That was where I'd flaunt my friendship with Jad in front of Milo, and rope him in even further.

It worked, too, of course: at the bash, I capitalized on Milo's slow willingness to drink, getting drunk as all hell with Jad in front of him by downing a copious amount of a disgusting green liqueur, along with everyone else at the apartment. By noon on holiday Saturday, all was blurry for me and for Jad, and for everyone else but Milo, who left to the sight of Jad and me passed out like puppies on my couch, numb and nuzzled into each other.

Milo gave me a new look, he flashed me a shockingly open expression in my office that following Monday. He was showing me even more of himself than I thought possible. He very directly talked to me about Jad. "Do you think he's a good kid?" Milo asked. And without even waiting for me to answer, he sliced himself open, his thoughts about his son oozing out everywhere. He felt a need to prove something about their relationship to me—as if a small glimpse at the untold depths of fatherhood should relay to me, definitively, that my friendship with Jad could not touch whatever bond they shared. There was this emotion, this competitive proving Milo was doing about the great well of his bond with his son, but there was also a genuine worry he was explaining, a worry that slowly overwhelmed any other theme of his speech to me on that heavy, hungover Monday morning.

"It's one thing," he said, "for you to get as shit-drunk as you do. I'm your boss, I see you here, I know what you're capable of. None of your nonsense interrupts your business, none of it detracts from your citizenship. But his, his partying, well, I don't know about its purpose, or its utility, rather—I can't say that partying has a 'purpose,' but I'm no genius about the morality of partying. Jad goes about his job, that web design work he does, as if there were no armada for him in employment. No battle. And, you know, I don't want to bring in too many war metaphors, but, as I've told you before, they're always unavoidable. There's a fight to be had, it's in shapes and wiggles and funnies—not in bullets and real blasts, no—and Jad seems afraid to have it. The way he takes to his work, it's as if he's giving a monster little platters of hamburgers, just to appease it, without actually fighting the monster. He'd rather that the monster was asleep. But you have to *take it to the beast*, you know that, I know that—and *your* partying is simply a decompression from all the load-up of the battle. We need these metaphors, we do—my tall father thought only objects could be real metaphors, but I assure you that histories can be metaphors too. A war, a trench to saddle into—that's what Jad is lacking. He parties like they're going to write a history of *that*, ignoring the fundamental flaw in his strategy; histories are written only for men who make the good stuff—money—come their way, and never for men who just spend it, who send it away from themselves. That's what the numbers are for, Bert—once you stack them, you can hurt folks with them. They love my numbers, and damn Jad hardly has any to work with. You know these things like I know these things, don't you now?" Milo waved his hands as if fanning a bad fume out of the area, and then he left my office without another word.

Five weeks later is when Larissa came into our office for a moment. When I heard her voice I was so terrified that I jumped from my desk and slammed the door to my office and locked it. I got down to the ground right next to my door, on my knees, and I cupped my ear to the space just beneath the door. I heard Milo introducing various banalities of the office to his wife, Larissa, and I sweated and sweated hearing the sound of her non-verbal replies. I didn't see her, not even for a second—I only heard she was coming in—and didn't hear her say a word on that day. She still wrecked me, though, she left me scavenged in all of my hearts with her presence, it depleted me to know about her, to know of her, I was losing my patience which had to grow larger, the plan had three months left until I could even touch her at all. That would be when I could make first contact on the supernova shape of her vagina, that landscape I trembled thinking of as I heard the levity and simultaneous weaponry of her non-verbal replies, her sensuously detached grunts, her mmm-hmms, as Milo showed her the office. I couldn't fathom a more exquisite creature than her, Larissa, her laugh was the laugh of the lies I told myself, the ones that would lead me inside of her.

I told Milo, as we approached May, that he and I should have a two-man "May Day rager," as I'd discovered at jobs past that such an occasion is one of the better times of the work year to get drunk as shit, to decompress, because there had been no celebration built into the calendar for some while, no holidays that didn't bore and didn't require church—something was needed to break the boredom, a true tonic to the malaise that gripped us as we approached May. My argument was not very good, but that didn't matter, for it was all a flimsy front for my charm. I invented this concept, this May Day rager, on a dime, because I'd walked into the office that day simply feeling too keen not to act. When I said hello to Milo that morning, I knew my needle was so much closer to his wound than it had ever been before. I was even taken aback by how close the needle then seemed to Milo's wound. He showed me far too much with his face that morning, with the way he freely putzed into my office wearing dejection, and clearly the kind that only a locking lover like Larissa could cause in him.

So he agreed, he was more than amiable to my intention of a May Day rager, it gave huge hope to his sagging face as I explained it to him, this rager with its many "beerings" and his Bulls playing on the TV screen. Milo had to wait a week for our rager, but it was already visibly difficult for him to hold on for that long. It was hard for me, too: I was seething with the want to know what Larissa had done to him, how she had brought him into this naked stumble he performed that morning. He was shackled by her somehow, she'd done another new thing to defy what he believed he could tolerate, she was expanding him in a way that was agony. I erupted inside at the thought of Larissa's viperous love, at the notion of her wonderfully narrow worldview, her sight for only what most disrupts her husband's stomach and forces him to vomit his dreams up and *come to the earth*, that thing he tried avoiding with his magic departmental code—the one I'd get from him—and with his special little basketball ballets he did in his precious little basketball room that Jad told me about.

No, Milo would not be the dancer, his tall tall father would hold onto that role forever, I'd remind him of that with the needle that I'd pin through his leg on our May Day rager, I'd make the first of the needle's insertions into the wound, if only for one moment, just to stab him down onto the reminder of his father, I'd insert the needle that way, I would.

And so it was on May Day, after a week of Milo's growing excitement, that I used Milo's enthusiasm against him. Three drinks in, I delivered my first blow, by saying I'd "always wanted to tap dance into infinity." Then I offered to buy shots, a whole flight of them in fact. "May Day is about catharsis, Milo. Catharsis and dancing all over this bar, weightlessly, that's what we need to do, we have to drink to the point that our merriment transcends the metaphysical and becomes physical. We'll take shots until we weigh nothing, let's go," I said to him.

Milo was frozen by how I evoked his giant dancing pap, knowledge he didn't know I had, and that he must have assumed I evoked coincidentally—he was stuck there like a stupid mule as I ordered the shots, he was slowly piping up and fakely saying how he couldn't wait, he was so thrilled, it was shot time, time to get these shots up in us and tip the bartender well, in the name of karma, we'd buy levity and karmic balance, we would.

Milo took the karma-tax shots and he started pounding his fists to the bar. After chanting "Derrick Rose! Derrick Rose!" for a while, he spoke of his father at length, mentioning more than once that he thought his father was a "man of great hate but also of great balance." Milo then said this, about his father: "He always wanted to chain me to things I ultimately wanted to be chained to, but I wouldn't let him, I'd go chain myself to something else, somewhere else, just to keep the metaphors between us straight. He and I would argue a lot about inane things as a way of arguing about important things. And the argument, it rarely ever happened through words. Once, for example, I became obsessed with toy trains. Specifically: toy trains that did crazy, annoying things, like winding around each room of the house, tooting incessantly and triggering a number of peripheral scenes, such as plastic firemen shooting water at plastic buildings, and plastic preachers preaching to plastic pew-kneelers. I wanted a huge-ass plastic society, of mine, to run through the whole damn house. For logistical, reasonable reasons, my father objected to these structures that my mother, initially, approved of and was delighted by. She hugged and kissed me from behind as I made them, as I wove a cohesive world through the house's architecture, creating what I believed to be—and what her excitement and love, I assumed, implied she also believed to be—an architecture that was complementary to the design of our home. My mother laughed and slapped her palms to the wall in wild affirmation as I said things like 'this is where the grocery store belongs' and 'this is how the mailboxes will be.' But when my father came home and saw what had happened, he smirked to no one, looking at the wall, very clearly away from me and my tizzied mother, to share something between himself and whatever that wall was to him, something like his God. I never believed my father bought all that Catholicism, especially not after I saw him do his damn dance, so his God must have been something as stitched-together as mine is. What filled him as he stared at that wall, condescending to my train construction with his Frankenstein-of-vague-notions God, was probably something my mother couldn't understand, I know that now in my memory of watching him stare at the wall, before he then destroyed my train world without laying a finger on it, and without asking anyone to lay a finger on it. That moment broke something, or it was at least my marking of something broken; it could've been broken before right then, I don't know, but I'm certain my mother couldn't understand my father's God, and that my mother's failure to understand my father's God was very similar to the way my father couldn't understand love, and that's what I understood to be the difference between tied-together men and women, and I still largely do see it that way, although it's quite the reverse and more perverse between me and Larissa, but we're outliers, that's what our love's all about, I assure you."

Milo looked to the ceiling as he said this bit, chuckling to himself in a way that made me so angry, but I wasn't about to tip my sleeve now and show him the fury of the needle, not just yet. There'd be a much better moment for that.

"Anyway," Milo said, "my father went on to never acknowledge or mention the system of train rails, and their corresponding scenery, and he never made physical contact with any of it either. He only stepped over it with a brilliant bodily language, a genius set of physical motions that absorbed all the psycho-emotional intangibles of our home, set into motion by my trains—my father, he maximized the nucleus of these psycho-emotional intangibles into a sort of daily ballet performance that was utterly persuasive, and completely painful, to both me and my mother. I'd see him using the fridge, holding to it and looking backwards over his shoulder to spot the perfect floor tile to step backwards onto, so to disrupt his equilibrium in an intentional way, and give himself excuse to stumble across the floor in a storm of elbows and knees that, somehow, seemed to make no physical impact but only a dramatic impact, despite my father's terrible size. My father, God's science experiment who gravity treated more favorably than it did other humans, disturbed no objects in his meretricious falling shows. The whole of the house and its encompassing trains remained intact after these shows of his, no booms, no bangs, only fireworks and clunkings of the theatrical kind. He would mention things just as he fell, sometimes, things unrelated to the train or to his subsequent falling, but things which seemed to tie a sickening knot around the train and his falling and around each of mine and my mother's actions. 'A man,' my father would say, examining the floor behind himself for the perfect balletic launch point, for the best place to start his spill from, freeing himself from the constraints of fatherly staunchness, allowing himself the realm of 'play,' I know that's what you say you love about my ping pong, Bert—*play*—but my father played in a stratosphere of shapes and dimensions I'm still not able to see. 'A *man*,' he'd say, 'should have a sense of avenue, he should have a compass, he should always have some good hunch with his way. I'm sure that the people he drives along would agree—his wife, his child, his clan should like it if the man leading them, well, if he can show you the way clearly and safely. Yes, it's a good thing to be firm and directional, rolling through the clearest and cleanest of paths, holding hands for some sentiment, everybody likes that,' my father would say, just before he began his tragic descent. The fall would usually begin with his left leg stepping backwards, so that he nearly landed his foot on the train track, but he missed it by a millimeter as he saw what he was doing and urgently corrected his step. His second left-foot step, the correction step, was then a pointed jab that sent him onto his cloud of an ass, on which he'd slide backwards across the floor, twisting his face into a macabre swirl and making a quick, almost girly little gasp of despair before he brushed himself off and stood from the floor, slowly and on his knees first, as if he were no longer the man we needed him to be, as if the right line were lost and our nonsense had led him to drive us into a madperson's house, a dangerous, dark place he couldn't help us in, he had no lantern in the dark and no weapon to protect us with.

"Of course, my father's cloud of an ass never left a trace on the floor—only on our hearts. It wrecked both me and my mother to see the man who housed us so convincingly perform the downfall of his competence. It showed us how his total decline of faculties was inevitable one day, he'd slip in his brain and his body like everyone else would and he showed you the trajectory, he gave you an aching preview of what his deterioration would be like, it wouldn't be possible to go on with life without him, our man. We couldn't watch this glimpse of his demise, it was far too terrifying to watch him so regularly fall. So my mother and I began reducing the trains gradually, then quickly, such that after a week only one small loop in the family room remained, hardly big enough for anyone to stand inside of. But my father stood inside it, he wouldn't let his dancing go, no, not yet, he hadn't taken all the trains away with his deft feet yet, he'd show you more of them, give you more of his tappy magic, his superb skills hadn't outmoded the train department yet so he brought his feet out once more. Only this time you could see him smiling a little—if my father can be said to have ever smiled, this would be one of those times that he smiled. But most wouldn't call it that. No, most would see the way my father's face looked as his legs turned to crazy wiggle sticks around the small train loop that evening and they would assume he was grieving. It's hard to explain the looks of my father's face, which may have never actually told me anything. I don't think my father liked having a face and I'm not sure he knew how to use one. But this was one of those times, like after those few chess games he'd grant you, that his satisfaction was known. My father's satisfaction, that most obscure, most furtive of feelings, it reared its head so clearly that night as he danced and did off the last of my train world," Milo said.

Milo asked the bartender if they had green liqueur, he said he was feeling nostalgic for something he'd never done, he wanted to suck shamrock goo down his face. The bartender said they had it, so I ordered a flight of shots of the disgusting shit, which disagrees fundamentally with the body, and Milo and I did the shots. We were drunk as all shit and leaning on each other at that point.

We went outside and got cigarettes from strangers, who were happy not to talk to us as soon as they'd paid their karma and lit us up. I sat on the curb, suddenly letting hubris get the better of me as I cackled a bit, remembering all of my new knowledge regarding Milo's feelings about his father. My charm, in combination with an intricate knowledge of Milo's daddy issues, would allow me to undo this man.

Milo asked why I was cackling and then he vomited green liqueur onto the curb repeatedly. I called for a cab on my phone as he was vomiting. I had to vomit myself, my body demanded a purge but instead I buckled myself in, I gave myself over to God's string and let the lord guide me back into the bar to settle the tab and return back outside before the cab arrived.

When the cab arrived I pulled Milo into my wings and I guided him into the car. That's when he said something that created a system shock to my whole plan, to my entire perception of the dynamic between myself and Milo, my victim who I thought until this point was my unknowing victim, but here Milo said something which put me into a spiral of doubt and confusion. "Do you remember Joe?" he asked, flopping into the cab with the smell of green liqueur vomit all over him.

In that moment, I nearly fell into Milo's arms and apologized to him, weeping. I almost trembled within his grasp and said I'd never think of it again, I'd never even mention Larissa to myself in my mind, not once, and I'd not ingratiate myself with Jad and his friends and I'd not hunt down his surplus of electronics store gift cards through false friendship and I'd not destroy him to learn his departmental code. I'd give up, I'd let him do anything for payback after my sin of deceit. I stood awash with this desire to surrender for too many moments before finally saying "Joe still works with us," closing the door, and running to the alley to vomit green liqueur profusely.

I took a cab home and when I woke I had a text message from Jad. It was about his cats, he said he needed a cat sitter. This, you see, was a rather important development for my plan, which was beginning to lose its original form and had started to take on a more gnarly, guerrilla shape in reality—I was in the trenches of my quest for departmental dominance and Larissa's vagina, I couldn't see the landscape clear anymore and I might have lost my terrific position with the needle, which had been right over Milo's wound. But this, this text message from Jad about watching his cats, this was a present from above.

"Bert my bro," Jad's text said, which I read with a throbbing headache. "Grizz and Dr. Shasta need your help. I'm going to Denver with my dudes and I thought you could look after them, they're the best girls there are, so I'm sure you'll like them bro. Come over tonight and I'll show you how to take care of my girls."

There was no doubt in my mind I'd accept the offer. To live as Jad, in his apartment with his cats, would be a role of inordinate value for me. There was no way I could turn this down. When I arrived at Jad's that night, he was pretending to ski, in anticipation of his upcoming Colorado trip. He threw his limbs about with glee, as if he were racing to death. "I can't believe anyone would do that insane deed; skiing," I said to him. Jad laughed.

"Bert my dude, I can't believe anybody's not doing it! It's like, man, it's a snow way whiter than that stuff we sniffed once." Jad then pretended that he had long, flowing hair while he pretend-skied, running his hands through the pretend hair the way that Milo did while he was playing ping pong, when he pretended he was Joakim Noah. "Girls!" Jad then said. "My *girls*!" he said, and both of his cats came running and they scaled up his dangling arms. He fell back with them and then Jad was wrestling with his cats, and this terrified me.

I can't be holding any needles over the wound, no, I lack almost any stillness or conviction at all if a cat is in the room; I don't trust those monsters, not a bit. So when Jad left the state for a week, to go "hit the slopes"—a phrase he used ad nauseam as I watched him perform cuddle pornography with his cats, for an hour, listening to him tell me how to care for his cats—when Jad left the state and was gone, I never let the cats gain good position on me again. When I visited to feed them, they often liked to dash up the kitchen counters (especially Grizz, that reckless bitch) and then leap onto a mantle that was high above my head. I'd immediately dart to the other end of the room when they did this, and I'd grab the loaded water pistol and point it at them; Jad had one of those little water pistols, the same that his father had at the January rager, it must be a family trait to love these sorts of bullshit childhood trinkets. "I can't give you the high ground," I'd say to the cats on the high-up mantle, who viewed me with falsely wide and falsely dewy eyes. I knew there was nothing but schemes and torture traps in those eyes. "I can never give you the high ground, so I'm here, and I've got that water you don't like. Don't pounce at me, and I won't shoot. And no, I won't be coming any nearer until you get down. I can see your plan, I know where that dastardly Dr. Shasta is and I don't trust her either. Shasta, PhD, she's got the order for me, I know she's somewhere in that darkness of unlit bedrooms just past the mantle. I know that even if I deal with you when I get closer, after you lunge from your perch to try clawing my eyes out, I know that then the doctor will deliver her terrible dose of surprise," I'd say, and I'd wait and point the pistol, and eventually the cute cretin would step down from on high. It often took long, though. The beast would even look around lackadaisically from its tower, attempting to lure me into a false sense of security, so I might move into her attack zone. “I know that you’re faking this daze,” I’d say, “I know because Shasta hasn’t emerged from those rooms, she’s still back there devising the perfect angle to assault me from—don’t think that I don’t know that.”

When Grizz finally came down from the mantle, one night, I took a more comfortable seat on a chair that I had put up on top of the kitchen table. Neither cat dared fuck with me on my makeshift throne, from which I enjoyed watching the rather pleasant details of their evil unfurl. I considered the possibility that they could understand me, first, and potentially communicate with Jad well enough in their gross cutesy wrestling patterns to let him know what I’d said, but then decided I’d do it anyway: I’d tell the doctor and Grizz about all of it from my chair of power. They bumbled about, often eyeing their paws as if they'd never seen them before, looking confused by all things—especially the string I'd given them and that they pretended to be perplexed by as they got tangled into it—but I still believed they were only trying to trick me into submission as they reimagined their possible strategic advantages over me.

"You'll never get me," I said to them. "You'll never get me—just like your grandpappy Milo never will. He'll be too busy watching his father dance in his soul to even touch me as I stick the needle in him, and then I'll stick my peedle into his wife. Yes, I want that heart-accelerating woman," I said to the cats. "She fills me up with a goo I've never had in me before. My wits are unusually challenged, you kittens, to come up with words to describe her to you. That Milo, yes, he's an amazing man to have won her, but the fun's over for him soon. Those Bulls of his will lead him into despair, he'll see, I'll count on them being there on his screen to divert him like that big, famous wooden horse, and I'll come diving out of his sporting club with the needle, I will, that's how it'll work. He keeps talking about these basketball playoffs and how they roil him, and I see how he burns for his father's untraceable love as he watches those dribblers, there's a ghost in him for that game. Not even creatures as devilish as you two could figure out what I've figured out, which is how to corral your grandfather Milo's exuberance about his Bulls squad, as they compete in the playoffs, into a critical-mass insecurity regarding my friendship with your daddy Jad. And to then leverage that insecurity into a series of tense episodes between himself and various employees—particularly Joe, you know—that then leads him to create an unlicensed 'sub-kitchen' in the spare office, as a sort of revolt against his own employees and employers. I will then reveal this 'sub-kitchen' to his bosses, and the big bosses will see this symbol of Milo's hubris and unacceptable eccentricity, and I will make it clear that I'm to be the man for the department, that Milo's strange departmental code, though still not entirely understood, is useless to our company now. 'You can't love this man's numbers when he's eating into company funds for this, for this disgraceful sub-kitchen,' I'll say, putting as much disgusted muster as I can into the phrase 'sub-kitchen.' By then, I'll also have Joe secretly on my side, and I'll compound Milo's bad standing by having Joe dredge up that old, life-destroying dish document to the big bosses. That forgotten deed, they'll remember it as I break the big bosses down with a sense of pathos for Milo's victim, hollow Joe will be standing lifeless and pleading before them, they'll see the shell, the emptied-out skeleton at your grandfather's feet and they'll see lies, all the lies in Milo's numbers. The digits are but a front for his fuckery. It will be then, during a confrontation I have with your grandfather, at his residence, that I touch his wife for the first time. I will stand outside his building with the loudest speakers I can afford, and play the song I once made love to in a loaded way. The harmonica, on this song," I said to the cats, then screaming the melody of the song's harmonica solo, leaping up and down on the table and using my hands to create an 'air harmonica' as I did. "The harmonica, it filled me with tin and gold and wheat as I lay there with my last lover, the one I don't care to see again but with whom I realized something about my life, which is that hardly anyone is watching it. Even Milo, the man I talk to the most, can't see even nine tenths of what it is that I do. No one would watch me have sex with this woman, this woman I didn't care about because I don't particularly care for women, not now anyway, just Larissa, but not other women. When the song played and I surged with the force of a comet as I ejaculated, full of that tin and gold and wheat, I began to embrace the shadows I lived in, I ran out on that woman quickly because who would ever know that I had—who would ever know that I've done anything at all? I'll play that God's-harmonica song, I'll blare it outside the residence of Milo, the man who I've just gotten fired from his post as my boss. He'll come to me, I know he'll come to me with those false wings of his and try flapping them at me in a frightening matter, but I see too much weakness in him, I'll merely dance, I'll run off this tap dance I've been working on and he'll die. I'll have been priming his mind for his pap in subtle ways for the better part of a year, by then, I'll have dug up the bulk of that trauma for him, put it front and center in his mind. When your man, your silly Milo, comes to fight me I'll fight him dead by dancing at his ass—I'll even bring up his old dead dog, I'll scream 'do you remember dead Frankie!' at him. And he'll cry, he'll fall over and Larissa will eventually come to him, that's when I'll put my descent into motion, my descent into her vagina by touching her in the special way, the way I realized while making love to that song is the pinnacle of intoxicants, was the most seductive way to touch a person, but surely I won't explain that to you cats, that knowledge is wasted on you, you're too busy figuring out how to make that string into a noose for me. You dumb furries, you can't hang me with such a ratty little thing. Don't bother trying, I'm too large for you, especially without your advantageous position on the mantle. Plus, by now I've figured out how to have you cornered with this water pistol right here, and you've got no way around me. And Larissa won't have any way around me either, no, she wont want to—she'll be shaking for me eventually, just not right away. Right away, she'll likely hate me, as I'll deliver my special touch only once she tends to her dying husband, the one I've killed with my dance, and she wont like me very much for killing him, and not for reaching into her deepest desires with my touch while I do it, either. But the seed, the seed I plant into her cavity with my touch, it will grow!"

I then threw the chair off the table, which startled the cats greatly—perhaps I'd made too much of them and their capacity for war. As the chair tumbled on the floor I shot the water pistol into the air, doing my murderous tap dance and gleefully feeling my shirt jump out of my trousers. "I've come untucked, kittens," I said. "I'm untucked Bert. Here comes the hurt, Milo," I said, absolutely loving the arc of my design, of my plot to destroy Milo and enter his wife, my seed wouldn't hatch for maybe months after my planting it but once my touch touched into her and the last of her nerves, she'd be mine, I'd have her and be the new holder of the department code, the new boss, the benevolent runner of the ping pong table and the laissez-faire administrator of the kitchen, the one and only kitchen, there wouldn't be any dissent, no, not on my time or the company's time, there's more than numbers to this, there's principles, there's rules of men and that's what Milo forgot, I'd let him see the cost of his miscalculating humanity so much, there'd be no dime not paid back on this onerous karma tax he's had coming.

This is what I thought, anyway, until the next week. Jad returned home from Colorado, and I met him at his apartment to return his key and confirm that his cats were alive and well. Jad incessantly told me stories about his skiing, that perilous folly, continuing to pretend that he was still skiing as he told these stories. I left his apartment and texted his father a picture of Jad with his kittens, a text sent for no reason of design, this wasn't part of the plan, I was just feeling ripe with the ability to cut Milo where it hurt—I could exhibit my closeness with his son a little more now, our special affinity away from his father.

The day at work after that, Milo was acting very strangely. He paced about the halls slowly and deliberately, muttering "Joe, Joe, Joe" to himself and often passing my office door as he did. I didn't make much of this, though, as he was passing everyone's office door. Milo was touring the office, muttering Joe's name all day, and anytime Joe came to him when he heard his name Milo would say "no, not you, Joe, just the idea of you, that's what I'm pondering," and Milo would say it without any harm—it was bizarre to hear him speak to Joe with no malice at all, and to also be evoking him so conceptually, as Joe stood physically before him. I did not understand why Milo would behave this way, or why anyone would ever behave this way, and it burned me; I envy too much that sense of play that he was again putting on. Milo seemed to send feelings out of himself forever and find completely new ones, it was as if he'd never hated Joe, not ever, and was only considering him as deeply as possible, to find the parable in Joe's life as it related to his own. "Not now, Joe," he'd say, with the utmost care, gently tapping Joe on the shoulder and proceeding on his contemplative tour of the office.

When I thought to confront Milo about his behavior, around noon, he beckoned me into his office, the one next to mine. It was rare that I entered this office, as mine and Milo's conversations usually happened in the hall, or in my office—almost never was I in his. It was magnificent in there, I admit; I hadn't been in there for at least a year, I tried to limit my exposure to his decadence, it was too painful, I was feeling myself wobble, woozy as I also imagined entering the cave of his wife's vagina, melting into a hopeless wisp, Milo was sucking me into it all along, pulling me toward his wife Larissa's netherly parts so to consume me with them, it was a trap! The windows of Milo's corner office showed this to me, I could see the sky all too much, it made me gasp like his falling father, I'd not seen the trains beneath my feet all along, he'd been building something against me for all these months—maybe years, maybe years!

Milo looked at me and asked me to sit down. "It's been a good quarter," he said as I sat. "The numbers have swollen even further for us, and I think we're due for a celebration. A surprise celebration for everyone here. Today. No more little electronics store gift cards. We're going bigger than that; no donuts, don't worry about your body in that way, today, Bert. What I think we're all due for, it's bowling. I think we've got to get out to the lanes today. What do you make of that idea, Bert? I'd like to be able to bounce even these things of seeming silliness off of you. Not just numbers and personal matters. I need a confidante in exploring the basic ways of keeping our employees happy, the numbers have been so good and we *need* a bit of merriment, so what does bowling mean to you; does bowling mean merriment, Bert?" Milo was nearly quivering with anticipation as he over-presented this idea of a departmental trip to the bowling alley to me. His mysteriously placid, contemplative pacing and muttering about the office all day, which frightened me greatly, it had apparently amounted to no more than the idea to go bowling.

"I think that's a terrific idea," I said with great relief. Milo then asked me to "rally the troops," so I took off my suit coat and threw it over my shoulder and said to Milo with false excitement that his "army will be assembled in short order." There was something about taking my suit coat off at that moment (something I'd never done before in this building) that was extremely satisfying and liberating. Standing across from Milo who sat at his desk, with my jacket off, this even gave me confidence that I could toe through those trains he'd been invisibly building all around my feet. Whatever advantage he thought he had, however many of my moves he'd anticipated, none of it could do enough to overwhelm my now even stronger charm, my coatless charm would be too much for Milo. I skipped about the office telling everyone to get to the lobby for free bowling, free pizza, free beer, there would be no more work today, this bowling bonanza was now what they'd all be paid for. My adrenaline increased as I gathered them all; I started to believe Milo wasn't so much ahead of me, that he was too myopic toward his strange, unpredictable code of running our office to actually even pay any mind to how I'd been advancing my plan to thwart his life and seize his job and his wife's vagina; her breasts; her face; her ass. I even spun my coat around over my head like it was a rally towel at one point, shouting "beer me!" as I galloped to the lobby when I'd told everyone about the afternoon's event.

I sat in the cushy lobby chair without my jacket on, waiting for the employees to gather near the elevator. Milo joined me. Standing before me as I chuckled in the chair, he danced a little bit. "It's bowling," he said, pretending to roll a bowling ball as the flourish to his spinning and wiggling. "I'll bowl you over, Bert," Milo said, laughing lightly, pretending to bowl again, sending his imaginary ball straight for my face, as if he were knocking over the pins of my joy.

This is when my mood sank again to fear, immediately; when Milo knocked over each tenth of myself with that imaginary ball, he knew just what he was doing, it was a strike, I'd been foolish after all, I was in too deep and couldn't handle this man's machinations. I kept that fear in me as the rest of the employees shuffled into the lobby, and as we jammed into elevators to take them downstairs to catch taxis. The seemingly random occurrences that happened just outside the building as we all hailed taxis to the bowling alley, I wondered in the car if they were random at all or if Milo had planned them, because I ended up in a taxi with Joe, just me and Joe, and it was a completely awful taxi ride.

I shook with the desire to mention the destructive dish document throughout the taxi ride, knowing that my desire was a direct result of my fear over what Milo might soon do to my soul. I thought that now was the time to get Joe on my side, as I'd planned to do, but my map toward taking down Milo and filling his life with myself, my map, it was all overthrown now, because now Milo had put me here in this taxi with Joe so that I would realize his grip was on me, squeezing me, he would have me stew in my failure. "Resolve," I thought to myself, "have yourself some damn resolve, Britwell. Extracting that man's blood with your needle was never meant to be easy, but your moves have amounted to something, even if he's doing so good a job of obscuring his holes at this moment. Have some fucking resolve," I thought, and then I broke the silence between me and Joe. "Quite the event," I said to him. "Bowling," I said, immediately despising my passive, dickless choice of words. Joe responded non-verbally; he merely mumbled a marginally affirmative noise, and not even in my direction, he mumbled this noise more in the direction of his window he was looking out —that's just how passive my words were, they didn't require even the dilapidated Joe to respond to them.

I knew I needed a better approach and I burned with the disrespect he'd just showed me, so I slapped my hand to the taxi's bench hard and I threw a twenty-dollar bill at the driver. "Pull over," I said, and the driver did, quite far from the bowling alley still. "But do not yet drive on," I said. Joe looked at me in confusion, and then I got out of the car and ran around to his side of it, and opened his door. I reached in to grab Joe, to begin sending him a message with my hands, but Joe shimmied like a little bitch across the taxi's bench, and went out the other door and ran across the street. I chased after him; the taxi drove off, and I wanted to curse at it, but there was no time to curse at it, not with the scurrying Joe off ahead of me by so much already.

Joe was a bad scurrier, though, his flapping legs looked almost tied together with his poor running form—I remembered Milo's

Bulls seeing this, I knew I had to insult his team's running form as part of my takedown, and so as I chased Joe I had new resolve to take Milo down, with the realization that I could pick apart his precious Bulls in this way. I quickly caught Joe, following him down an alley between two hotels, and when I caught up to him I grabbed him and pushed his back against the cold stone wall.

Joe said he didn't want any part of this, he said to beware of Milo, he said he could tell I was running right into Milo's sharp, toothy mouth with the way I was behaving. I wasn't as sleuthy as I thought, Joe said, and he said that I didn't look any good without a jacket on, either, and then Joe was laughing—a resigned, insane laughter poured from him. "He'll take it all away from you, all of it, but he'll also make you stick around," he said.

And then Joe walked off, howling with more of that laughter, and I let him walk off.

Then I myself walked multiple miles to the bowling alley, slowly. When I got there, I saw Milo and the rest of them in the pizza parlor, shoving unhealthy trash into their faces, and I went to their table and tapped Milo lightly on the shoulder, attempting to remind him of his pap, this was all that I had left.

Milo turned around and said "Bert! Britwell! Where have you been! Come to the bar with me, come," he said, and then he pulled me with him as he skipped to the pizza parlor's bar, far too glad to be alive in this mediocre hole that smelled like gestate diabetes and looked like broken hopes. He ordered us each a shot, and we took it, and then he said "I bet you didn't think I knew about the sub-kitchen plot," visibly resisting the urge to cackle as he continued. "I see you more than that one tenth of the time that you think is all, that you think is total," he said. "You see, I've brought my numbers with me again, to hurt you with, it's a much higher percentage than that ten that you mentioned, but I won't tell you just how much I've investigated, or just how much I've perfectly predicted your realities with my imagination, with this mind you can't fathom. Bert, it's not yours, it's mine. You thought there was nothing in my donut consumption inventory, in my handling of Joe, in my love with my wife and my son, but in these things there is a spine you can't see, a whole God-structure of dancing stars making up a constellation far above your head, I could never explain to you how all of this works, it would be far too embarrassing for the both of us. But suffice to say, at base of how it all works is the brutal fact that I'm clobbering you with right now—it's the numbers, Bert, they're still here and still receiving great big love from the great big bosses, by the men who matter, I can see you quaking under the weight of my math. Now, we'll be friends and you'll drop these things. Don't try any of it, I promise it won't go Britwell for you," Milo said, now no longer holding back his urge to cackle. "Come, come with me," he said, pushing me with his evil wing toward a vacant booth in the mostly vacant pizza parlor, the place of my fall.

"I want to play a game with you," he said as we sat. I was silent and I was trembling, and he grabbed a salt shaker and began to pour salt onto the table. "This one is called 'blow the salt,' and I've just invented it right now, but it's also an old favorite." Milo poured a hefty little pile of the stuff onto the table, and blew at it gently, such that it took about ten seconds for the salt to even move as he blew it, but when the salt did move, it scattered like slow snowfall. "You might think there's nothing arranged about these little specks," Milo said as he blew, "but that's the difference between you and me. Here, here I see not the random spill that you and that dipshit of a waitress inevitably will, no, I see a strata of great fate. Salt, shit, whatever it is: it doesn't end up where it ends up for no reason. You, Bert, you're not here for no reason. Listen up, because this is what you'll need to understand for your next go-around—for I hope there'll be another go-around; I'd be so disappointed if you didn't give me another run with your little tricks, you've got to get them bigger, you've got to emerge from the trenchcs more valuable, man. What you don't see in this dance of ours are all the underlying things. Pry all you want into so-called logic, look for the code I use in my big-boss-endorsed dominion over all of you, but you will never contain my decisions and behavior into a chart that can project what the next maneuver will be. That's what it's all about—my nose takes me where no one else smells a thing, the numbers don't come from other numbers, they come from my instincts. They're a consequence of my animal grasp on you all, I'm the king of the hill, I've barked you all down with ease and now you're making me bark you down a little more theatrically than I'd like to, Bert, I do know that this is a bit much. But I'd be lying if I said I didn't cherish this crushing, either. Come, come my crushed," Milo said, gesturing to the scattered salt, "come and blow the salt a little yourself, won't you?"

As he asked me this after his doggy diatribe, I realized Milo was getting a bit ahead of himself. I might not have had the needle right over his wound like I thought I did, but there was still a wound—there's always a wound—and I still had enough left in me to get at it. I grabbed a butter knife from the napkin roll on the table, and I placed it like a border on the table, just below Milo's chest, and blew tidily at the salt. It all clumped up at the edge of the knife, and then I swept the whole pile to the center of the table, and reduced it, with more sweeping of the knife, into the smallest pile it could be. "This one," I said, sliding a good fourth of the stuff to its own section, "this one is your pap. He's my primary weapon against you. Regardless of what you know of my plans and my knowledge of your father, I'm sure that you're not ready for my full-on assault on your daddy issues, which are clearly immense. Mine are too, because I'm a boy like you're a boy, but you don't know a thing about my father because no one in this city does. Not a thing. Not even close. And this one," I said, creating pile number two, "is your Bulls, your pitiful Bulls, that team lost in their malaise these days, don't think I haven't been keeping tabs on that squad and noticing how it affects your mood. In fact, I'd even say that your sudden action toward me today is all about the Bulls' recent struggles. I can see their problems forcing your hand, causing your overzealous stupidity."

Milo then swatted the table with fury, and the salt flew all over. "Look!" he said. "Look! Now your piles are everywhere again! You no longer know a thing, not without your silly organization, you can't make a shape from the disparate realities that compose our life, no, you've got your calendars and plans—ha!" Milo said, standing now and pointing at me. His face was very red, and a few co-workers began to take notice across the room. "You don't know what it's like to run with my wife, how it feels to have her urges dictate your body! This is the post-game show!" Milo shouted, then leaning over to grab the salt shaker from the table and unscrew its top off, staring at me. "You've already been defeated, I've driven into the lane and dropped the ball-bomb into the hoop of your heart, you're already dead this time around, Bert, I'm just telling you how I did it." Milo then poured all of the salt onto the table recklessly, and dropped the shaker from maximum height. "Clean that up or I'll turn you into Joe," he said, and he stormed off, out of the pizza parlor, waving his arm to beckon the rest of the employees to join him near the lanes.

So I swept up all the salt, into one pile, as the employees trotted after him, eyeing me with skepticism and fear. I swept the whole pile into my palm, it was a ridiculous amount of salt, and I ran after Milo. "I'm Bert, here comes the hurt!" I said, and poured the salt down the back of his shirt. Milo then shook and screamed in horror as the employees around watched in a state of shock. I rubbed the salt through the back of his shirt, saying "right into the wound, right into the wound!" and Milo turned around and tackled me to the floor.

I laughed deliriously as he got up and took a bowling ball from the nearby racks. "You're going to bowl with me now," he said, "you're going to bowl with me for your job, and you're going to do it *my way*."

I said "alright, my Milo," still laughing deliriously, pulling my sore bones up off the floor. "Let's have a bowl, Milo," I said. "Let's bowl. Let's *play*, like you do, that's right, I'm finally ready for a bit of a play. Let's make a day of nonsense and garbage, let's masturbate into the ether, finally, play, it's time for nothing, for vacuous crap, I get it, sure," I said, shaking with giggles as I grabbed my own ball. Milo was so furious that he pretended to throw his ball at me repeatedly, shouting noises that weren't words. The employees all shrieked in fright as Milo did this, they believed he was actually going to throw it at me, but I didn't believe he would, I just laughed relentlessly.

I proceeded to throw a strike in my first frame, and point at Milo and shout "right into the wound!" with glee, but he then threw his own strike, and we then traded three suspenseful frames of equivalent, sub-strike scores as the employees all watched us silently. We were tied in our game and I was laughing and Milo was not; our dispositions had somehow been reversed!

"This is your way, is it?" I asked Milo, the automatic ball-return machine between us. "Doesn't seem like you're proceeding with too great a sense of play, today, are you Milo? You're taking this quite seriously!" I laughed as I said this, and he scowled at me and went to grab his ball, but I put my hand down on his preferred ball—a bright pink ball, to be sure; perhaps this was the last remaining refuge of Milo's so-called proclivity for play, this queer color choice—and I held the ball down with everything that I had as he tried to grab it from under my hand.

"Let's play my way!" I said madly, and then Milo slapped me as hard as he could in my face and he climbed over the machine and shoved me. "You can never be me!" he said. "You're not me! Stop trying to consume my person, you can't have it, you can't have my job or my woman," he said. He shook his finger in my face as he convulsed in rage, and he clutched my tie. He told me that I didn't look any good without a suit coat on, and I shoved him back, and then we got into an argument about height, about who was taller.

After some of that, I realized the truth, the empirical truth, and I yelled "I'm taller!" with utter conviction and leaned back recklessly while Milo still held my tie, such that his holding my tie was the only thing keeping me from falling and hitting the parquet floor behind me. So I karate chopped my tie and I let myself fall, and the employees all emoted surprise as I continued to laugh and laugh, and then I scooted my butt backwards on the parquet for a while before getting up and doing my dance, the tap dance that I'd built to kill Milo. "I'm taller!" I said, wielding this fact like Milo does his precious numbers, I said it over and over again, "I'm taller, I'm taller!"

Milo was obliterated by my dance. He cried, and then he screamed, and then he threw a bowling ball at my feet but I hopped over it and it flew toward innocent, anonymous bowlers who jumped out of the ball's way. An extra hop even came into my motions as I almost effortlessly dodged Milo's toss, I was a true dancer now, and I started making my way toward him with my act, I inched this savage display closer and closer to his crunching heart, and he fell to his knees and moaned, he was helpless in the face of my traveling terror. The wound, it was his heart, his only heart, and I had the needle calmly right above it. I was just a moment from pinning Milo's heart to Bert's bulletin board, and staking a glorious claim in Chicago for some time, I could stay here.

Just as I was almost next to Milo, though, with all the employees and most of the bowling alley's denizens watching the pinnacle of our showdown, Larissa entered through the bowling alley's doors. I saw Larissa and I died a death worse than whatever my tap dance could do to Milo, I panicked severely, and I barely even saw that behind her, there were police officers, the fuzz. They'd come for any number of reasons, I suppose, but as I panicked I ran for Larissa, because I saw it all crumbling underneath me, every piece of my vaunted plan, and I quickly decided that I had just one chance left, only one, to deliver my terrific touch.

Larissa, amidst the red-and-blue lights flashing through from the parking lot, widened her eyes. I had to touch her but I never touched her. The fuzz swallowed me as I sprinted toward her, and the whole of my dance died in a blaze of bastard striving as Milo howled on the parquet floor and his woman went to him. As I was taken away, the fuzz hit me in my gut and I vomited nothing near the bowling alley's doors, I'd not eaten that day so I heaved nothing but my hopes as they dragged me away.

Made in the USA
Monee, IL
19 January 2021

55957891R00069